Puffin Books

Two Village Dinosaurs

Surely one dinosaur was more than enough for any village! But when another dinosaur was hoisted up from the depths of the chalk-pit, the Parish Clerk's worst fears were realized. Even if young Jed Watkins was looking after them, two dinosaurs spelled disaster for the Best-Kept Village competition, destruction at the village fête and double trouble in every way. Dino and Sauro trampled their amiable way through the village, causing chaos and confusion on every side. However, even dinosaurs can be useful sometimes, as the Parish Clerk was about to find out!

This funny and charming story continues the adventures begun so successfully in *The Village Dinosaur*.

Phyllis Arkle also wrote the very popular *Magic at Midnight* and *Magic in the Air*, both now in Young Puffin.

Two Village Dinosaurs

Phyllis Arkle

Illustrated by Eccles Williams

Puffin Books

Puffin Books, Penguin Books Ltd, Harmondsworth,
Middlesex, England
Penguin Books, 625 Madison Avenue,
New York, New York 10022, U.S.A.
Penguin Books Australia Ltd, Ringwood,
Victoria, Australia
Penguin Books Canada Ltd, 2801 John Street,
Markham, Ontario, Canada L3R 1B4
Penguin Books (N.Z.) Ltd, 182–190 Wairau Road,
Auckland 10, New Zealand

First published by Brockhampton Press (now Hodder & Stoughton Children's Books Ltd) 1969
Published in Puffin Books 1981

Made and printed in Great Britain by
Richard Clay (The Chaucer Press) Ltd,
Bungay, Suffolk
Set in Monophoto Plantin

Contents

1. A companion for Dino

Fancy finding *another* dinosaur hibernating in the old chalk-pit – a companion for Dino! Jed Watkins couldn't get over it. Using two cranes and slings, workmen had managed to lift this colossal animal out of the layer of fine sandstone in which it had lain for millions and millions and millions of years. Jed had immediately named this animal 'Sauro'.

Jed looked round at his father, warden of the village recreation ground, who was standing among the crowd of villagers.

'Look, Father!' he shouted, his voice shrill with excitement. 'Sauro is smaller than Dino, but I bet you could drive a tractor between his bandy legs without actually touching him.'

'A small tractor, perhaps,' Mr Watkins agreed smiling.

Sauro, warming up by a bonfire, shook himself and rose slowly to his feet. Dino moved forward and Sauro seemed delighted to see him. Their great long necks swayed to and fro above the crowd and they prodded each other with their small snake-like heads. The sudden noise of aircraft flying low overhead did not disturb Dino, but Sauro raised his head and probed the air at this unknown danger. His muscles rippled under the hide and his tail twitched nervously.

'Will he be all right, sir?' asked Jed
anxiously, turning to Mr Holloway, his
headmaster.

'Oh, yes, yes, I'm sure he'll soon settle
down. Animals are just like people. They
don't take to change at first. Give him
time. Remember a modern world must be
a confusing and frightening place for a
dinosaur.'

The Parish Clerk was standing near
Jed. His face wore a solemn, worried look.
He'd grown quite fond of Dino, but the

thought of having to put up with the antics of yet another dinosaur was upsetting.

He called out to the laughing, jubilant crowd. 'It's all very well, but have you thought of the extra food needed – to say nothing of shelter for the winter? And if this one is anything like Dino, there'll be trouble sooner or later, mark my words!'

The villagers paid no heed to him.

'You'll see!' he shouted. 'Anyway, we'd better get them along to the recreation ground. Some people seem to have nothing to do and all day to do it in. Lead the way, Jed. Dino will follow and let's hope Sauro will take the hint.'

Jed walked on ahead, whistling. Dino raised his head and listened. After allowing time for the order to sink in, he followed meekly after Jed. Sauro, long, tapering, whip-lash tail churning the mud, also moved forward very, very slowly. The Parish Clerk, Mr Holloway and Jed's father kept pace with Jed. The villagers followed the dinosaurs, keeping well away from Sauro's well-armed feet and tail. They knew it would take time before the new arrival trusted humans and became reliable. It was a very long procession.

People who had been unable to go to the chalk-pit leaned out of windows along the street. One or two waved flags. Some made do with dusters. They called to one another.

'We'll have the television people here again.'

'And the reporters.'

'And the press photographers.'

'Isn't it fun!'

But the Parish Clerk didn't think it was so funny. 'You'll soon stop laughing when you're told there'll have to be an extra penny on the rates, "for the upkeep of dinosaurs". I know you ratepayers!' he cried.

Sauro, ambling along behind Dino, peered over hedges and walls. Then, something attracted his attention. Unfortunately, it happened to be the rose-bed in the garden at the side of the Parish Clerk's house. Everybody was forced to halt. People a long way off in the rear of the procession craned their necks, wondering what had happened.

Sauro swung his long supple neck over the hedge, bent his head and slowly sniffed at the roses. His soft teeth pulled at a beautiful yellow rose, which slowly disappeared into his mouth. Then, carefully avoiding the thorns, he took another and yet another.

'Food is the first thing an animal needs,' observed Mr Holloway.

But the Parish Clerk was very put out. 'Oh, what a calamity! Dino ate all my prize marrows and now Sauro's going for my roses. I'll have nothing, absolutely nothing, to exhibit at the shows. And all because of these two dratted dinosaurs. How I wish I'd never set eyes on either of them!'

Mr Holloway chuckled. 'Things will

liven up enormously now we have *two* dinosaurs. We must expect a few casualties here and there. Such is the price of fame!'

'Wait until Sauro gets at your delphiniums. You won't be so pleased then,' retorted the Parish Clerk.

'Oh, but he won't bother with my delphiniums. Once he's developed a taste for roses, he'll stop at nothing to get at them.'

'Sauro will soon learn to behave, sir,' called out Jed, anxious to keep the peace. 'Dino doesn't steal much now he's got used to his vegetables.'

Jed ran on ahead. 'Come on, chaps, nearly there,' he encouraged, whistling furiously. Sauro reluctantly withdrew his long neck and followed Jed and Dino down the lane.

'Watch out for the fence, Jed! We've only just repaired it after Dino's efforts,' bawled the Parish Clerk.

But it was too late. Dino stepped gently through a gap in the fence like an elephant that has learned to use its feet carefully, but Sauro trampled on the fence and crushed it into the mud.

The Parish Clerk covered his eyes with his hands and Mr Holloway said, 'It's no use, Mr Parish Clerk. We'll have to take down this section of fencing altogether for a time, otherwise we'll be putting it up, taking it down, putting it up again – it's not worth the trouble.'

The Parish Clerk groaned. In fact, he'd done a lot of groaning ever since Dino had first been dug up out of the pit. No one took much notice of him now. 'If only we could get rid of them both, I'd be a much happier man,' he muttered.

Mr Holloway spoke firmly. 'You know you don't really mean that. Dino belongs to us and now we have Sauro as well. They're both ours.'

'He'll be no trouble at all, sir,' said Jed optimistically.

'No trouble!' echoed the Clerk, thinking of Dino's frequent, usually disastrous, outings.

'No trouble at all,' repeated Mr Holloway confidently. 'Moreover, we must get ready for a greater interest in our village. Never fear, Dino and Sauro will pay for their keep.'

'I hope you're right,' exclaimed the Parish Clerk.

Dino made his way to the side of the new hall where food and drink were laid out for him. Sauro followed, rubbing shoulders with his companion. He sniffed at the food uncertainly. Jed picked up a large cabbage and, pulling it apart, offered a few juicy leaves to the dinosaur. Sauro slowly sucked them into his mouth and began munching. He evidently liked the taste for he took some more. When he had finished, he lowered his head to the stone horse trough and noisily took a long drink.

'Teaching an animal to eat food he's not used to needs a lot of patience. That's where you will come in, Jed,' said Mr Holloway.

'I hope Jed will be able to persuade Sauro to leave my roses alone,' said the Clerk. 'And, another thing, the milk will cost far too much. We just can't afford it.'

'Oh, Dino drinks very little milk now, sir. I've been adding more and more water to his diet. And I'll take them into the lanes so that Sauro can eat dog-roses.' Jed was determined to put the Parish Clerk's mind at rest.

'That's the idea,' said Mr Holloway approvingly. 'Don't start Sauro on milk. What he never knows, he'll never miss.

They'll both thrive on water. And make sure Sauro eats some honeysuckle as well as dog-roses. Keep him sweet!'

Jed's school friends were rushing about gleefully. Not another village in the whole world owned one dinosaur, let alone two. Suddenly, one of the boys pointed down the lane and shouted, 'Here they come!'

The Parish Clerk shuddered when he saw the television vans turning into the lane. News certainly travels fast. There was no peace nowadays. And why, oh why, had it rained last night, making the ground so wet and soggy underfoot? He was thinking back to the day Dino had arrived. The hubbub ... reporters and photographers rushing about ... cables trailing ... grass trodden down ... mud everywhere ... the paddling pool a dirty brown colour!

It was happening again and he couldn't bear it! Despairingly, he turned towards the village hall. He went through the open double glass doors and sat down heavily on a hard wooden chair. Then he put his head in his hands and waited until it was all over!

2. The Best-Kept Village competition

Jed stayed close to his two charges as the reporters and photographers – and the villagers – crowded round. Such a commotion had never before been heard in the village, not even when Dino had arrived. There was more noise than when the annual fête was being held on the recreation ground. It was getting very late when the last van bumped down the lane and everyone, tired out, decided to go home. Jed was left with his father and Mr Holloway.

'You'd better go and tell the Parish Clerk it's all clear, Jed,' suggested Mr Holloway. So Jed went into the hall and tapped the Parish Clerk on the shoulder.

'They've gone, sir,' he said timidly.

The Clerk was still in a stupor. He got up slowly and went and stood outside the hall. His eyes, missing nothing, roved all over the recreation ground and then rested finally on Dino and Sauro. 'Still eating, I see. Their jaws never stop working!' he said indignantly. 'And just look at this ground!'

'The dinosaurs have to eat a lot to keep their enormous bodies healthy,' said Mr Holloway reasonably. 'And don't bother your head about the ground, Mr Parish Clerk. It won't take long to get it really ship-shape again.'

But the Parish Clerk wouldn't be pacified. 'I'll tell you something,' he said. 'We won't get any further in the Best-Kept Village competition. The judges will be visiting us again any day now. And to *think* we were in the "possibles" list for the first time. I had high hopes of reaching the finals.' He sighed. 'But look at this ground – never seen anything like it in all my life. And think of my garden ...'

'Don't worry,' said Mr Holloway again. 'First thing in the morning, I'll go along to the nurseries and buy some flowering rose-bushes in containers to replant in your garden.'

'And I'll tidy up this ground so that you won't recognize it,' promised Mr Watkins.

'Oh, and I'll do anything, *anything at all*, to help, sir,' offered Jed eagerly.

Mr Holloway and the Parish Clerk went home and Jed, helped by his father, made sure Dino and Sauro were comfortable. Mr Watkins had to laugh as he watched his small son's figure disappearing from view as Jed walked round the great squatting beasts. The dinosaurs certainly took up a considerable amount of room!

'Hurry up, Jed. It's getting very late. High time you were in bed,' Mr Watkins called out as he walked off across the ground to the cottage.

'Won't be long,' answered Jed. Sauro's hide looked dried-up and dusty, the result of long hibernation. Never mind, Jed knew that dinosaurs liked, more than anything, to be in water. Dino had got into the habit of bathing daily in the river and, no doubt, Sauro would do the same. Jed wasn't worried. Sauro would be all right.

He gave the animals a last look-over before running off home, thinking how lucky he was to live right on the recreation ground, so near to where the dinosaurs were quartered.

Jed went willingly to bed. When he crept out early next morning and stole a look through the window, there was no sign of the animals. He dressed very quickly and was out of the house before his parents had awakened. He ran through the village, over the bridge and down on to the river bank, laughing out loud when he saw four ears sticking up out of the water like submarine periscopes. Several ducks, tails flapping, were keeping well out of the way.

'Out you come, Dino, and you too, Sauro,' he ordered. He whistled and waited. He was used to waiting. Eventu-

ally, Dino's neck rose up slowly like a
conning tower and Sauro's followed.
Their tails floated on the top of the water
as they walked towards the bank. Dino
lowered his head for Jed to tickle behind
his ears. One day Sauro will do the same
thing, thought Jed, looking fondly at the
two great beasts lumbering out of the
water.

The village was already stirring as Jed
led the animals back through the street.
Any day now the judges would be coming
for the second time to inspect the village
for the Best-Kept Village competition.
There had been great activity during the

past few weeks. Gardens and grass verges had been tidied and window boxes replanted. Some shop-fronts had been repainted, the war memorial had been scoured and all the inn signs had been cleaned.

The Parish Clerk, like a general in command, stood on his front doorstep, looking sharply up and down the street for the least trace of litter or untidiness. Jed wished Dino and Sauro would hurry. Their large bodies nearly filled the street and their heads reached over the rooftops. They ambled along at snail's pace. When the Parish Clerk saw them, he ran forward waving his arms and shouting, 'Get those beasts back to the recreation ground, Jed.'

As they drew nearer, he grew more agitated. 'Oh, mercy on us, look at all the mud they're bringing with them and those blessed water weeds again. These beasts are a positive menace! You'll have to keep them on the recreation ground until the judges have been round again.' He clapped his hands loudly at Sauro as the animal turned his head towards the rose garden. Jed was really thankful to get the animals back home.

Jed and his friends spent every spare minute with the dinosaurs. Then school broke up. And how better to spend one's summer holidays than looking after two placid prehistoric monsters?

As Jed had foreseen, Sauro followed Dino down to the river every morning and cooled his bulky body in the water. One morning when Jed returned from the river with Dino and Sauro he was delighted to find several bales of straw propped against the village hall.

He called out to his father, busy with a roller, 'I'll get them bedded down really comfortably.'

'That's right, Jed,' replied Mr Watkins, pausing from his labours for a moment. 'Make sure they've got enough food and water, and always see they're as clean as possible.'

Two Village Dinosaurs

There wasn't nearly enough straw for such large creatures, but Jed and his friends did the best they could, spreading a quantity on the ground before Dino and Sauro squatted down. Jed ran off and returned with a pitchfork, with which he carefully frisked up the straw all round the dinosaurs. 'They look just like two swans on a nest,' he chuckled.

'Fat swans!' laughed Mr Watkins, coming to take a closer look.

The Parish Clerk came down the lane, calling out as he drew near Jed. 'I thought it was a good idea to have the straw delivered and I hope these beasts will be content to stay here quietly today. I have a feeling the judges are coming this afternoon. The streets have been swept clean and my garden looks much tidier with the new roses. I'll brook no nonsense from Dino and Sauro this time, *so keep them away from the village this afternoon!*'

'Oh, you can safely leave Dino and Sauro to me, sir,' replied Jed confidently.

'I'll keep them here all afternoon.' When he was alone with the animals, Jed wagged his finger at them. 'Now, you heard what the Parish Clerk said, so don't dare move,' he told them. 'I'll be keeping an eye on you both.' He ran home. Several times during the midday meal he got up and went to the back door of the cottage, from where he could see the dinosaurs.

'For goodness' sake, Jed, don't leave the table again until you've finished your meal. Take my word for it, those two great lumps of mischief are far too comfortable to move off again just yet,' said his mother.

'They only think of eating, drinking and sleeping,' put in his father. 'What a life! Wish I had a job like that.'

After the meal, Jed helped his mother. 'Can I go now, please?' he asked, when the last dish had been dried and put away.

'Oh, all right,' she replied. 'Off you go. I can't think what you found to do before those two creatures came into our lives.'

Jed ran out – and stopped short in horror.

'They've disappeared!' he yelled.

Mr Watkins, who was having a much-needed nap, was very annoyed. 'What's that? Gone, you say? Good heavens, Jed, go and find them before the Parish Clerk sets eyes on them!'

Jed's short legs covered the ground at record speed. He followed a trail of straw. There were strands blowing gaily about

in the breeze before festooning the trees, and strands trodden down into the gutters by giant feet. As Jed rounded the corner into the street, Dino's tail was disappearing over the river bridge, but Sauro had stopped outside the Parish Clerk's house and was making a meal of the new roses.

Jed hung back guiltily when he saw the Parish Clerk's plump figure, spectacles pushed back on to his forehead and newspaper in hand, appear at the front door. The Clerk let out a roar that brought Mr Holloway rushing out of his house on the opposite side of the street.

'Great Scott, Mr Parish Clerk, you did give me a fright. Whatever's the matter?' asked the headmaster.

'Matter? Matter? Can't you see – my roses – all this straw!' His voice rose to a shriek. 'Those two horrible hefty monsters are at it again!'

Sauro was enjoying the roses. Had his brain been larger than a hen's egg, it might have occurred to him how kind it was of the Parish Clerk to keep providing him with such delicacies.

As it was, the Clerk was nearly beside himself, and when he looked up the street and saw Jed cowering in a gateway and, beyond him, two men appearing round the corner, his rage knew no bounds. He jumped up and down, threw the newspaper on the pavement and stamped on it. 'Here come the judges,' he hissed. 'This is more than I can bear.' He turned to Sauro. 'Be off, you great thieving monstrosity!'

Sauro decided to leave a few roses for the next visit and his bulky figure shuffled off down the road after Dino. The Parish

Clerk, breathing heavily, watched him go.

'We'd be much better off with ten elephants,' he sighed. 'They wouldn't take up any more room, and at least we'd have the ivory of their tusks to sell. As it is, we might just as well own two useless mountains with a long tail and neck attached to each.'

The two judges came up to him. 'Fine beasts, those two dinosaurs of yours,' one said admiringly, watching Sauro's tail disappearing from view. 'Never seen anything like them before.'

'Nothing in the whole wide world resembles them, believe me,' said the Clerk.

The judges strolled up one side of the street, looking all around them, and came back down the other side. They opened out their marking sheets and consulted together.

'Street tidiness?' and shook their heads.

'Absence of litter?' They pursed up their lips and frowned.

'Tidiness of gardens?' They cast their eyes at the Parish Clerk's garden. 'Not a very good year for your roses, is it?' commented one.

'Well, we'll just take a look at the recreation ground,' he continued. 'Perhaps we'll find an improvement there,' and off they went, tut-tutting to themselves.

The Parish Clerk, straws sticking out of his hair, heaved a great sigh. 'Ah, well, that's the end of that. We'll be scratched from the "possibles" list. There'll be no cup for us.' He looked at Jed and then stared hard at the headmaster. 'And if anyone dares to tell me again that those two gigantic, lazy, over-fed useless fiends are going to *earn their keep*, I'll ... I'll ... I don't know what I'll do! You ought to be helping me get rid of them, instead of always saying how valuable they are to us.'

3. Dino and Sauro in the film

Just as the Parish Clerk turned to go back into the house, a large, chauffeur-driven car drew up. The door was opened and out stepped a tall, smartly-dressed man. Jed crept forward shyly. He recognized the film director who had wanted to buy Dino.

The Parish Clerk looked back. 'Good afternoon,' he said sourly. 'Fancy anyone visiting a "Bottom of the list for the Best-Kept Village competition" village – and all due to those two dinosaurs. I wish with all my heart I'd sold Dino to you. I expect you've heard we've got another one now?'

The visitor didn't answer immediately. He looked eagerly up and down the street. At length he said, 'I've got a proposal to put to you which will bring in a nice sum of money.'

'Anything to do with dinosaurs?' asked Mr Holloway, grinning. 'They're not very popular around here at present.'

The director laughed. 'Well, in a way,' he replied.

'Good old Dino,' exclaimed Mr Holloway.

'Good old Sauro,' echoed Jed cheerfully.

But the Parish Clerk was still truculent. 'I don't believe those two great barrels of destruction could be of help to anyone,' he scowled.

'It's like this,' explained the director. 'My company is making a film about medieval times. Now, the mud and straw have given this street an old-fashioned look – just right for one of the scenes in the film.' Stepping into the middle of the road, he gazed up at the roofs of the houses and shops.

The Parish Clerk's face had brightened, but now he said gloomily, 'I know what you're thinking. There weren't any television aerials in those days.'

'True, true, but what's to stop us dismantling them for one day?'

'People would never agree,' gasped the Clerk. 'They wouldn't be able to look in at their favourite programmes.'

'Phooh! We'd get a move on with the filming and they'd only miss one day's entertainment. *And* we'll pay five pounds to each resident as compensation for the loss of viewing.'

So the Clerk and the director interviewed all the householders, who readily agreed to the suggestion. (Especially when they heard about the five pounds!)

'That's very satisfactory,' said the director. 'If it suits you, I'll be back in a week's time to start filming and I'll keep in touch with you in the meantime.' Taking one last look up the village street, he said, 'Good afternoon,' to everyone, waved his hat at Jed, got into the car and was driven off.

Everyone gathered round for a conference. The headmaster turned to the Parish Clerk. 'How's that for the dinosaurs "earning their keep"? There's no money in a Best-Kept Village competition cup. This is much better.'

'Of course it is,' agreed the Clerk. 'Haven't I always said the dinosaurs are a credit to the village? We're indeed very, very lucky to own two such fabulous beasts and don't let us forget it.'

Jed glanced at Mr Holloway.

'But there's one very important matter

to be decided,' continued the Parish Clerk. 'How on earth are we going to prevent the dinosaurs charging up and down the street while the filming is taking place?'

'Oh, really, Mr Parish Clerk, do be accurate!' remonstrated Mr Holloway. 'The dinosaurs are quite incapable of lifting all four feet off the ground at one time, let alone charging up and down.'

'Well, anyhow, they've got to be kept away from the street. Now, Jed, what are *you* going to do about it? No one else has much control over those two beauties. Are you prepared to stay with them all day and miss the fun?'

'Oh, yes, sir, I don't mind missing the filming. I'd much rather stay with Dino and Sauro. I'll get them down to the river and back again at crack of dawn. Then they'll be content to stay on the recreation ground for the rest of the day. They'll be very well behaved, I promise, sir.'

'All right, then, that's settled. Whatever

happens, *keep them out of the village on that day!'*

A week later, Jed got up very early and fed the dinosaurs. Then he led them through the village and down to the river. He watched as they waded in until only a few feet of dinosaur necks were exposed.

When Jed thought they had been in long enough, he gave the signal for them to come out. He waited ... and waited ... and waited. Nothing happened. Time was getting on. Poor Jed! He whistled until he was blue in the face. Then he took off his shoes and socks and waded into the river as far as he dared, calling to the two animals.

Eventually, Dino decided to move and rose very slowly out of the water and came towards the bank. Sauro followed. It was a frustrating journey back for Jed. He had to hang about while the dinosaurs ate the leaves off the topmost branches of a tall tree, and again when they stopped to gaze – at nothing at all!

The Parish Clerk was already out and about. He would be, thought Jed. 'Hurry up, for heaven's sake, Jed,' he said fussily. 'It's getting late.' As though it was all Jed's fault.

Mr Holloway came out of his house. 'Good show, Jed,' he said approvingly. 'Just in time.'

As Dino and Sauro made their way home, the first motor in the convoy of vehicles belonging to the film company drove into the village. Jed heaved a sigh of relief.

'Now Dino, and you too, Sauro, just settle down for the whole day,' he encouraged in a loud voice, his head flung back so that he could peer up at them. As a special treat – or was it a bribe? – he fed them some bread soaked in milk, although he well knew that was now forbidden. And the animals settled down to chew.

Jed wasn't bothered about missing the filming. Dino and Sauro had taken to him more than to anyone else. Oh, yes, indeed, he would miss *anything* to be with them. He wasn't going to leave them this time. Oh, no! His mother had provided him with sandwiches and a bottle of orange squash. And at intervals a friend ran down the lane from the village and described what was going on.

'The rooftops look very strange without the aerials and the road is covered with wet straw and muddy pools – just like old streets we've seen on films!'

Later on the news was, 'The cameras have been set up on gantries and the actors and actresses have changed into medieval costumes. It's wonderful! There's been nothing so exciting in the village since Dino came along.'

The day wore on and Jed had no more news, because no one came to visit him. He could hear shouting and, occasionally, the clip-clop of horses' hooves. He started to fidget. Dino and Sauro appeared to be fast asleep. They'd curled themselves up

40

with heads on long necks tucked in towards their bodies. They didn't stop
munching, however, and bits of leaves
stuck out from the corners of their mouths
alongside their whiskers.

Jed leaned over and rubbed his hands
over Dino's neck, talking to him sooth-
ingly. 'I *told* the Parish Clerk you'd be as
good as gold. Can't think why he gets so
angry. This village would still be going
on in the same sleepy old way if you hadn't
been discovered.'

Jed ate the last sandwich and noisily
sucked the remains of the orange squash
through straws. Then, chewing a piece of
grass, he got up and strolled about, kick-
ing at a loose, grassy sod. He walked right
round the two massive beasts, deciding
that it was a distance of a quarter of a mile,
or – at least – one eighth of a mile. And
when he stood between Dino and the wall
of the hall, it was as dark as being in a
tunnel.

His footsteps took him a little bit farther

away, in the direction of the village, as a matter of fact, and a little farther still. Not for one minute did he intend leaving them. Oh, no! As he rounded the corner he glanced back. Dino and Sauro were sound asleep.

Jed hardly recognized the village. Men, women and children in period costume were standing about on the pavements and a man dressed in a smock was waiting to push up the street a rickety old hand-cart piled high with vegetables. Old-fashioned baskets, as well as iron pots and pans, hung from hooks outside some of the shops.

The 'stars' stood ready in the doorway of the inn, and the director, seated on a tall stool near to the cameras, yelled through a microphone, 'That's perfect. Get ready for the final take.'

Jed was thrilled with it all. But, suddenly, he felt the earth tremble. He'd had that sensation before. Broad, padded feet were plodding towards him. They'd moved! At first, he was proud because they had followed him, but then, when he thought of the damage they might do, he was horrified.

Cupping his mouth in his hands, he shouted at the top of his lungs. 'Wait a minute, sir, please don't shoot yet. Dino and Sauro are coming! I'll drive them back.'

But once on the move Dino and Sauro came on like a couple of slow-moving bulldozers. Jed was forced to walk backwards in front of them, and the Parish Clerk, hair fringing his bald head standing on end, kept step with Jed and tried to halt Dino, who was in the lead as usual. The villagers were enjoying themselves and cheered from their vantage point on a raised terrace, out of the range of the cameras.

Losing his balance, the Parish Clerk fell over backwards and rolled into the gutter

out of the way of the dinosaurs' feet. The
stars ran hurriedly into the inn, while the
extras slipped and fell about in the roadway. The handcart was knocked over and
all the vegetables rolled about in the road.

'Take!' ordered the director, breath-
lessly. The cameramen, eyes bulging, took
no notice of him. 'Take! Take!' roared the
director again, standing on his stool in

order to get a better view and shaking –
as Jed thought – with rage. So the cameramen filmed the scene of pandemonium
and turned their cameras hastily on the
dinosaurs as they drew level.

As can be imagined, the Parish Clerk,
helped to his feet by Mr Holloway, was
in despair. 'I knew this would happen. I
just *knew* it!' he cried. 'Trust those two

to spoil everything. "Earn their keep" did you say?' he asked Mr Holloway. ' "Well behaved" did you promise?' he sneered at Jed. 'We'll be charged for spoiling the film instead of being paid for cooperating. *And* we'll have to pay for the vegetables – look at those two hulking brutes now!'

Dino had discovered the vegetables rolling about in the roadway. He helped himself to a few and then, as there wasn't room for two dinosaurs abreast, moved on ahead to allow Sauro to have his share. Jed was crestfallen. Everything had been ruined and it was all his fault. He turned hesitantly to the Parish Clerk. 'I'm very sorry, sir,' he said. 'I'm to blame. I shouldn't have left them, not even for a single minute.' He couldn't resist adding, 'They followed me.'

The Parish Clerk rolled his eyes skywards. 'Ah, well,' he moaned. 'It's only to be expected of those two prodigies of ours, I suppose. But I'll never get used to them, *never, never, never,*' and he stamped his foot three times in emphasis.

The director came running up. To Jed's surprise, he was shaking with mirth. 'What's the matter with you all?' he cried. 'Everything's fine, just fine. That film will make a gorgeous comedy "short". Haven't seen anything so funny for years. People slipping all over the place, vegetables rolling into the gutter. And those two gargantuan beasts! Cheer up, do, Mr Parish Clerk. I'm prepared to pay you an extra fifty pounds for that film. It won't take us very long to get the street prepared again for the proper filming. No real harm has been done.'

Mr Holloway smiled at Jed as the director continued. 'Now, then, Jed, do you think you can get Dino and Sauro down to the river – they're headed that way – and keep them there for a while?'

'Oh, yes, sir, I'll see to them,' sang out Jed, already on his way. 'Come on, Dino! Hurry up, Sauro!' he shouted. After a lengthy pause, Dino sauntered after Jed.

Sauro raised his head, a large cabbage dangling from his mouth, and decided to follow.

Glancing back, Jed noticed a broad grin on the Parish Clerk's face! Perhaps, one day, the Clerk would *really* appreciate Dino and Sauro.

Jed put on his 'thinking cap'. Now, what could the dinosaurs do to make the Parish Clerk really grateful? Something *very* helpful?

4. Dino and Sauro at the fête

Next day, Jed was still thinking how Dino and Sauro could really impress the Parish Clerk. Now, what was worrying the Clerk more than anything? He'd got it – money! That was it. Dino and Sauro could help to raise funds at the annual fête next week, couldn't they? Next time Jed met the Parish Clerk, who was talking to Mr Holloway in the street, he told him about his idea.

'Get people to pay *five pence* each to view those two bloated beasts? You must be mad, Jed. In any case, don't forget they'll tower over everyone and everything on the ground. No one will want to *pay* to see them.'

Jed felt hurt. Fancy anyone saying things like that about the dinosaurs. 'Yes, I know everyone will be able to see them, sir,' he replied. 'But visitors might care to have a close look at them. I thought of roping them round and letting in a few people at a time.'

Mr Holloway was more encouraging. 'A trench would be the only sure method of keeping the dinosaurs captive,' he said. 'But, on second thoughts, it would have to be such a whacking big trench, it would take a gang of workmen about a week to dig one!'

'Those animals take up far too much room as it is,' said the Clerk.

'But it's not a bad idea of Jed's to rope them in,' continued Mr Holloway. 'We need a really good profit at this year's fête. As you know, the community hall is costing far more than the budget.'

'You never spoke a truer word!' answered the Clerk.

'And it would be disastrous if it should rain,' continued the headmaster. 'You wouldn't take my advice and insure against a wet day.'

'Stuff and nonsense! It's never yet rained on fête day. I'm not going to be bitten like that – paying out good money for insurance when it isn't necessary. I wasn't born yesterday,' cried the Clerk.

He turned to Jed. 'All right, then, young fellow-me-lad, do what you like with those two darlings of yours, but two pence a time is quite enough for anyone to pay.'

'Should be two pounds a time,' muttered Jed, under his breath.

The sky was cloudless on the morning of the fête. After the dinosaurs had had their early morning bathe, and had settled down by the hall, Jed and his friends got busy. Plenty of straw was laid down, green vegetables were to hand and the trough was filled with water. Jed's father had provided several coils of rope, with which the boys fenced in the two stupendous exhibits.

Hands behind his back, the Parish Clerk strolled round the ground, supervising everyone. Last-minute checks were being made on the model railway and the fun fair was ready to go. The Parish Clerk stopped near the dinosaurs. A large notice met his gaze:

FIVE PENCE TO COME CLOSER TO
THE GREATEST BEASTS ON EARTH,

it read.

'It should read,

TWO PENCE TO VIEW THE
GREATEST NUISANCES ON EARTH,'

exploded the Clerk, turning to a rebellious Jed.

At two o'clock, many anxious glances were cast up at the darkening sky. 'Only a passing cloud,' said the Parish Clerk reassuringly.

'I sincerely hope so,' replied Mr Holloway. 'But it's a very, very big cloud and it's taking a long time to pass over.'

As soon as the ceremony of 'opening the fête' had been performed, Jed and his friends started doing a roaring trade. There was already a queue waiting to get nearer to the greatest beasts on earth. Jed took the five pence pieces eagerly. He had always loved fête day – the smell of candy floss and hot dogs, the music and the milling crowds.

Dino seemed to revel in all the attention, but Sauro was restless. Ears pricked, he turned his head this way and that, towards music coming from the bandstand and the blare from the fun fair. He seemed to be on the alert all the time for the first sign of danger.

The 'queen' was due to be crowned at three o'clock and the film director, floral crown in hand, stood beside her on a small wooden stage especially erected for the occasion. The Parish Clerk, looking very important and grand, was also on the stage with the committee.

Unfortunately, just at this moment, Sauro decided he had had enough. Before Jed realized what he was up to, he had moved off, breaking the ropes and pulling the posts out of the ground as he went. He glanced uneasily at the roundabouts and flicked his tail contemptuously towards the model railway. People fled in all directions as he made for the stage. The Parish Clerk jumped down hastily and ran forward.

'Oh, no! Oh, no!' he screamed. 'Jed, where are you? Head him off! We're just going to crown the queen.'

'I'm here, sir,' panted Jed, running right underneath Sauro's stomach. Sauro was now near enough to the stage to stretch out his neck and go after what had attracted him – brightly coloured, delicious-looking flowers, including roses! Before the director realized what was happening, Sauro had nibbled at the edge of the floral crown. Snatching it away quickly, the director put it behind his back. But he was no match for Sauro, who butted him in the ribs.

The director gave up. Laughing heartily, he placed the crown firmly on the top of Sauro's outstretched head. 'I hereby crown you "Queen of the Fête",' he shouted through a microphone.

The Parish Clerk was simply appalled. Never before had anything so disgraceful happened to him. He would never live this down. The shame of it – and the real uncrowned queen running crying off the stage!

Sauro seemed very annoyed. He tried, without success, to shake the crown off his head. But, no matter, he had noticed more flowers. The fact that they were on the head of a plump committee lady didn't matter. He bent his long neck and daintily took the hat from the head of the astonished lady. Turning, he trundled off in the direction of the village, one floral hat dangling from his mouth and the crown perched on top of his head. Dino decided to follow him.

'Wait until I get my hands on you, you thieving, ugly ruffian! I'll show you ...

I'll give you what for ... I'll ...' The
Parish Clerk's agonized voice fairly rent
the air.

Jed hurried off and wandered un-
happily round the fair ground. Such a
pity. He could have taken a lot of money
and the Parish Clerk would have been so
pleased. Ah, well, perhaps he'd be able to
think of something else. But he'd have to
allow the Clerk time to get over this un-
seemly episode.

To add to Jed's misery, the rain started to fall and it wasn't long before it became a deluge. The band struggled on dismally, but were eventually forced to cover their instruments and run for shelter. A few youngsters were determined to spend their pocket-money, so the fun fair carried on for a time, but they too had to give up. It was a sorry end to fête day.

With hair plastered over his forehead and rain trickling down his neck, Jed stood forlornly outside the officials' tent. His father looked out and saw him. 'Come in here out of the rain, Jed,' he called.

'Pity you didn't take out that insurance,' the headmaster was saying mildly to the Parish Clerk as Jed crept into the tent. 'We would at least have had that much compensation money.'

'Never mind about the insurance. What about those dratted dinosaurs making such a mockery of the whole thing?' cried the Clerk. 'Whoever heard of a dinosaur being crowned queen! We'll be the laughing stock of the whole country. That reporter of ours will have sent the news to the national press, trust her.'

He paused, glaring balefully at two policemen, who had appeared at the tent opening. 'Oh, come in, do,' he shouted. 'More trouble? Well, I'm resigned to anything these days.'

'Anyone round here own two dinosaurs?' asked the sergeant, keeping a straight face.

'Not them again! Oh, no! Break the news gently, please, I feel weak.' The Parish Clerk sat down heavily on a canvas chair, which promptly sank into the mud and deposited him on the ground. Jed rushed to help him on to his feet again.

'Come on, tell me the worst,' spluttered the Clerk. 'I suppose I'll have to take the blame the same as usual. Why ever did I agree to keep them? They'll have to ...'

'Oh, no, indeed, they won't have to go,' put in Mr Holloway quickly.

'Well, what have they been up to? Let's hear it,' ordered the Clerk.

'It's like this,' began the sergeant. 'This afternoon, just as two gentlemen – in a hurry, they were – emerged from a certain building in the main street of the village, Sauro comes strolling along. He had something on his head. I don't know what it was.'

'It was a crown,' muttered the Clerk.

'A what?'

'Oh, never mind, do go on.'

'Well, the din of aircraft passing overhead startled Sauro, who lurched to one side, pinning the two men against the wall as they rushed out of the building.

'They were terrified. We heard their shouts and screams for help down at the police station,' said the policeman, shaking his head. 'It was pitiful.'

'Oh, dear me, how shameful,' said the Clerk, a hand to his lips to stop them trembling.

'That's not all!'

'I don't think I can bear any more today,' murmured the Clerk.

But the sergeant went on relentlessly. 'A few yards farther up the road a high-powered car was parked alongside the pavement.'

'Well, what happened to that?' asked the Clerk fearfully.

'Dino comes along. He prods Sauro, who moves forward, leaving the two men prostrate on the pavement. Another jet streaks across the sky. Sauro bumps into the car, crashing it against a wall, trapping the driver inside the car.'

'And I've never heard anything like *his* shrieks. Terrible!' added the policeman.

'I don't want to hear any more,' pleaded the Parish Clerk. 'We'll be sued for heavy damages, I know. Let's hope we can afford to pay them.' He turned to the headmaster. ' "Earn their keep" did you say?'

Mr Holloway was stroking his chin thoughtfully, in the way Jed knew meant something had occurred to him. '*Which* building did you say the men were leaving?' he asked.

'I didn't say, sir,' replied the sergeant, grinning from ear to ear. 'I was waiting for someone to ask me that. It was the bank.'

'But it's Saturday,' replied Mr Holloway. 'The bank closes at 11 o'clock.'

'Exactly, sir. These men were unwanted clients, bank robbers, in fact. Thinking everything would be quiet in the village, most people being at the fête, they gained entrance to the bank through a back door. They overwhelmed the bank manager and clerks, who were working late. Then they collected all the money and made their way out through the front door, where the car was waiting for them.'

He heaved a sigh of great satisfaction. 'I can't tell you how proud our small

61

police force is to have had a hand in capturing three cunning and dangerous criminals.'

'And all because of Dino and Sauro!' burst out Jed, unable to keep quiet any longer.

'All because of those two lovelies,' agreed the sergeant. 'Full credit must be given to them for capturing the thieves.'

'A good day's work,' commented Mr Holloway. 'I'm only sorry it turned out such a wet day for the fête.'

'Oh, bother the rain,' shouted the Parish Clerk exuberantly. 'Let's go and see if those animals are all right. What a boon it is to own two such intelligent beasts.'

'Come on, Jed,' said Mr Holloway, patting the boy on the shoulder. 'You're certainly bringing up your two charges to be very helpful.'

'They're always willing, sir,' answered Jed, with satisfaction. 'They're the cleverest animals, as well as the largest, in the world.'

'I agree to the latter statement, Jed,' smiled Mr Holloway. 'But as to being the cleverest, well, I have my doubts – but they'll do!'

5. The Professor arrives

One day, after school, Jed was looking after Dino and Sauro, spraying them with a hosepipe and rubbing parts of them within his reach with a hard-bristled brush. Looking up from his task, Jed saw the Parish Clerk, letter in hand, approaching across the recreation ground.

The Clerk had been very pleased with the dinosaurs lately. In fact, he was more enthusiastic about them than anyone else in the village. 'How fortunate we are to own two such magnificent beasts. I wouldn't be without them for anything,' he would say. Jed hoped everything was still all right.

The Parish Clerk waved the letter in the air. 'I've got something here that will interest you, Jed,' he called out. He gazed at the dinosaurs. 'I'm glad you're taking such an interest in their appearance. They're growing into fine-looking animals.' Glancing down the lane, he continued, 'Ah, good. Here comes your headmaster. I'd like him to hear me read this letter.'

Mr Holloway came up to them. 'My word, Jed,' he said. 'The dinosaurs are in

fine fettle. Sauro's hide has lost its dingy look. And as for Dino – well, he positively glows with health.'

'There isn't a finer beast in the whole world, sir,' said Jed. 'Or a better-natured one.'

'Or a faster-moving one – I don't think!' The Clerk laughed boisterously. 'But, seriously, I agree with you, they're in excellent condition and you wouldn't find better-behaved animals anywhere.'

Mr Holloway raised his eyebrows and Jed hastily agreed. 'You wouldn't, sir, oh, indeed, you wouldn't.'

'Which brings me to this letter,' continued the Parish Clerk. 'I was just going to tell Jed, Mr Holloway, that I've received a communication from a Professor Klott, who lives in a town in eastern Europe – one with an outlandish name. What *do* you think the silly ass says?'

Mr Holloway and Jed shook their heads.

'I'll read it to you – the silly idiot! – just listen to this: "News has reached me that you are the owner of two so-called dinosaurs, the same having been dug up alive out of a chalkpit. I feel it my bounden duty to inform you that, in my opinion, the animals are *not* dinosaurs, there having been no such creatures on this planet for over 200 million years. In my opinion, they are giant lizards of a type common in New Guinea. As I shall be in England next month, I hope you will permit me to visit your village and prove my theory".'

'Giant lizards – look at them!' scoffed Mr Holloway. 'They're dinosaurs every inch – every yard, I should say – of them.'

'Lizards. Best joke this millennium,' roared the Clerk cheerfully.

'Well, they belong to the same family as lizards, but that isn't what the Professor means,' said Mr Holloway.

'Let him come,' cried the Clerk contemptuously. 'We'll give him the shock of his life.'

'He'll certainly be surprised,' commented the headmaster, smiling at the two animals, whose heads were towering over the roof of the community hall.

'The dinosaurs have been doing splendidly lately, one way and another, but we could do with more publicity, especially abroad, and this may be the means of getting it,' said the Parish Clerk.

'Keep up the good work of grooming them, Jed,' advised Mr Holloway.

Jed needed no urging although it was hard work. His father helped him to make a trench for the water to drain into after the animals had been hosed down daily. 'They like lots of cool water in summer, as they can't stand extremes of heat or cold,' Mr Watkins explained.

The Parish Clerk and Mr Holloway often came along to keep an eye on the dinosaurs. 'We may be able to make capital out of this business with the Professor, and then we can begin to think seriously about shelter for them before the winter,' announced the Clerk.

'That's a "must", I'm afraid,' replied Mr Holloway. 'I doubt very much whether they would be able to stand a severe winter without some kind of protection.'

'Hm,' said the Clerk. 'Well, if they earn enough they'll merit a shelter.' He smiled at Dino and Sauro.

Jed spent all his spare time caring for the animals. 'We hardly ever see you these days, Jed, except when you come home for meals and sleep,' complained his mother.

'Oh, but Dino and Sauro must be in really first-class condition when the Professor arrives,' replied Jed proudly.

Early one Friday morning, the Parish Clerk came running down the lane. 'The Professor will be here tomorrow, Jed,' he cried. Jed looked up from his task of preparing the dinosaurs' breakfast. The

69

Clerk went on, 'He hasn't given us much notice, has he? But, never mind, he couldn't see two finer-looking, better-cared-for animals anywhere, thanks to you, Jed. Tell your father, will you, before you go to school, and I'll go along and give Mr Holloway the news.'

That evening, Jed and his father gave the animals a thorough grooming. Jed was so excited he could hardly sleep that night. In the morning, when he went out, there was no sign of the dinosaurs. They'll make their own way back from the river, he thought.

But when he met the Parish Clerk and Mr Holloway in the village, the Clerk said, 'I think it would be advisable if you got them back to the recreation ground straight away, Jed. It's going to be very hot today and they might take it into their heads to stay in the river.'

'It would be funny if we had to say to the Professor: "There they are, four eyes, four ears and two noses," ' laughed Mr Holloway.

'I'll go and fetch them,' said Jed, running off towards the river.

He looked upstream, he looked downstream, but he couldn't see any sign of the dinosaurs. He waited in case they had submerged completely for a brief spell. But no, there wasn't a ripple and the fallen leaves lay motionless on the glassy surface of the water.

Jed was very worried. Perhaps they were in the thicket alongside the railway line? He ran off to continue the search, but there was no trace of the dinosaurs anywhere. Reluctantly, Jed rushed back to the village and arrived breathless at the Parish Clerk's house.

'I can't find them *anywhere*,' he cried, very near to tears.

'Can't find them? Oh, no! Oh, no! They can't have disappeared again!' He flayed his arms about like a windmill. 'Get a move on, Jed. Do something. Find that couple of troublemakers at any cost.'

Poor Jed ran home. He told his father and mother what had happened. 'No peace, now,' sighed his mother. But his father said, 'Now, don't worry, Jed. They've been missing before and we've always found them.'

'Yes, I know, but there isn't much time. The Professor is due here in an hour or so.'

All the boys in the village turned out to help in the search. They spent all morning looking here, there and everywhere, until they were tired out. Jed felt his legs wouldn't support him much longer.

When they finally arrived back in the village, there was a small group in the street. The Parish Clerk and Mr Holloway were talking to a tall, thin, supercilious-looking man wearing a light mackintosh and a trilby hat with a feather stuck in the side. The Professor, thought Jed!

The Parish Clerk
was very, very angry.
'Don't believe me,
you say? But everyone
here can vouch for
Dino and Sauro.' He
spread out his arms
to include the curious
villagers crowding round.
'That's all very
well,' snorted the Professor.
'But where
are these animals? Don't tell me creatures
of the size you claim they are could vanish
into thin air. If their necks are so long,
how could they hide? Are they afraid of
me, me, the mighty Professor Klott,
world-authority on all kinds of reptiles?
Tell me that, are they?'

Almost nose to nose, the Parish Clerk
and the Professor glared at one another.
The Professor hadn't finished. 'Now, I
had expected that at least there would
have been a band playing to welcome me

73

– and a procession led by the so-called dinosaurs!'

Jed saw the Parish Clerk clench his fists and hold his arms rigid at his sides. The Professor was going too far with his taunts.

But Mr Holloway was stroking his chin. 'Procession, did you say?' he murmured. 'Procession?' he repeated loudly. 'That's it! Come on, Mr Parish Clerk, and you too, Professor. And you, of course, Jed. Jump into my car and I'll take you to see the two greatest phenomena on earth.'

'I hope you're serious, Mr Holloway,' cried the Parish Clerk, still shaking with rage and mortification. He climbed into the back of the open car with the Professor, and Jed leapt into the passenger seat beside the driver.

Mr Holloway drove towards the nearby town. Jed was hopeful, but mystified. There was no circus in the town to steal the dinosaurs. What had Mr Holloway in mind?

74

As they entered the main street of the town, they could hear music, and crowds of excited children and grown-ups lined the pavements. A policeman came forward and held up the traffic.

'Hear anything, Professor? The band's approaching and the procession won't be long in following,' smiled Mr Holloway.

'It's University Rag Day!' shouted Jed suddenly. 'The students must have kidnapped Dino and Sauro in the night.'

'Here they come, Professor! Here they come!' The Parish Clerk stood on the seat of the car and threw his hat up into the air. It fell down into the crowd and was lost for ever.

First came red-coated bandsmen, led by a drummer, playing stirring music. They were followed by several colourful 'floats'. Students in all kinds of costumes ran about rattling tin collecting boxes under people's noses. The Parish Clerk waved them away. 'No, no, no. You ought to be paying *me*,' he cried.

Then came the dinosaurs. 'Dino! Sauro!' shouted Jed at the top of his voice. 'I'm here. I'm here.' The Professor's eyes fairly boggled. He hissed through his teeth in amazement. The Parish Clerk dug him hard in the ribs. 'Is that a dinosaur, or isn't it?' he asked. The Professor moistened his dry lips and nodded and nodded and nodded.

Suddenly, everything was forced to halt. Dino had recognized Jed. His long, long neck came down towards the car. The Professor, and the Clerk – who had never quite got used to the dinosaurs – scrambled out in a most undignified manner. Everything was in a state of confusion. As usual, however, Mr Holloway took command.

'I'm afraid you'll have to lead them back home, Jed. We'll follow in the car,' he said.

The crowd cheered and roared as the massive beasts passed down the street. The powerful tails thrashed about a little, but Jed knew that Dino and Sauro had lost their fear of humans and wouldn't lash out dangerously. The Professor, back in the car, was overwhelmed. 'I'd never, never, never have believed it if I hadn't seen them with my very own eyes,' he kept saying over and over again. 'What a tale I shall have to tell when I get back home.'

'Well, I told you all along they are dinosaurs,' said the Parish Clerk complacently.

The Professor departed that evening full of apologies for not believing that Dino and Sauro were really dinosaurs, and he promised to make amends by spreading the news all round the world.

Next day, the Parish Clerk, Mr Holloway and Jed were on the recreation ground, discussing the previous day's events, when two shamefaced students arrived. They said they were very sorry they had kidnapped Dino and Sauro. 'But we thought they would be such an attraction and bring in a lot of money for charity,' one student said, in justification.

'That's all very well,' fussed the Parish Clerk. 'But what about the money it costs us to feed, to say nothing of trying to house them?'

'Well, we've heard about the dinosaurs needing a shelter for the winter,' the student continued. 'So we've all clubbed together – there are a lot of us – and we've bought a disused hangar for them, which we hope you'll accept.'

'A hangar?' cried the Parish Clerk, aghast.

'A hangar?' laughed Jed. 'Just the very thing. They'll both be able to get in comfortably and snuggle down in the winter.'

'A hangar? That's a good idea,' smiled Mr Holloway. 'I'm beginning to think you're right, Jed. The dinosaurs are clever – in their own way. At least, they've earned themselves a cosy home for the winter.'

'They're not doing too badly,' agreed the Parish Clerk. 'But I can't imagine what an ugly contraption like a hangar is going to look like alongside our brand-new community hall.'

He *would* have to say something like that, thought Jed disgustedly.

6. Dino wins the race

Jed wished the Parish Clerk wouldn't go on so about the hangar spoiling the look of the new hall. What did that matter so long as Dino and Sauro were comfortable? Trust the Parish Clerk to make a fuss about nothing.

Mr Holloway had a suggestion. 'Why not site the hangar on the out-of-use allotments? The ground might as well be used for something.'

The Parish Clerk gave the matter some thought. Then, 'Not a bad idea,' he cried. 'Not a bad idea at all. I'll discuss it with my council at the next meeting.' The council voted in favour of the proposal and, in due course, the dinosaurs' new home was erected on the old allotments, a little way down the lane from the village hall.

All the villagers and several students from the university turned out for the opening ceremony. It was a very gay occasion. Everybody cheered as the Parish Clerk opened the doors of the hangar and, led by Jed, the dinosaurs strolled into their new quarters, snuffling all round before finally settling down. The hangar was very roomy and high enough for them to get in easily, so long as they lowered their heads, which they quickly learned to do.

The Parish Clerk announced that he was very pleased with the new accommodation. As though *he'd* provided it, instead of having grumbled about it, thought Jed indignantly.

'Now, when we want to keep the dinosaurs out of the way, Jed, it'll be simple,' boomed the Parish Clerk. 'Just settle them inside the hangar and close the doors.'

Keep them hidden away! Fancy *anyone* not wanting to see Dino and Sauro. Jed couldn't believe the Parish Clerk was serious.

'Next week is a case in point,' continued the Clerk. 'As you know, royalty will be passing through this village on their way to the races. At all costs, the roads must be kept clear of ordinary traffic then. That means those two mischief-makers will have to be kept in their quarters. Too risky even to allow them down to the river. They'd only do something daft.'

'But won't they want to see Dino and Sauro?' asked Jed, astonished.

'No, no. They're only passing through the village. Mind you, if we're lucky they might, at some future date, make a special visit to view the dinosaurs. That would be something. My word, we'd be famous all right then.'

On the day of the races – a school holiday – the village was bedecked with flags and bunting and looked very gay in the sunshine. Police were on duty controlling the traffic. Everybody turned out. The village was spick and span and the Parish Clerk was very pleased with it all. Only one thought saddened him. 'What a pity it isn't judging day for the Best-Kept Village competition,' he sighed.

'Some people are never satisfied,' retorted the headmaster.

'Dino and Sauro tucked away comfortably, Jed?' called out the Clerk jovially.

He didn't wait for an answer, which was

just as well. Dino and Sauro were *not* in the hangar. In fact, Jed hadn't the least idea where they were. He'd been down to the river, but there was no trace of them there. But he wasn't bothered. He knew from past experience they'd turn up eventually. So long as they didn't put in an appearance before the royal cars had passed through the village!

Jed quailed at the thought of the huge bodies blocking the street, holding everything up. Sauro would probably go for the elegant hats on the ladies' heads. And how embarrassing that would be.

There was a stirring among the crowds lining the pavements and Jed put such awful thoughts from his mind. Soon, the first car, standard on the front gaily fluttering in the breeze, came into view, slowing down as it passed the cheering crowds. Jed waved his flag as energetically as the rest.

When the last car had disappeared round the corner, Jed and his friends began to look for Dino and Sauro. But there was no sign of them anywhere and Jed began to get really worried. It was nearly 12 o'clock and the search had to be abandoned.

After the midday meal, Jed said to his father, 'I don't want to go to the fair this afternoon. I'd much rather stay and look for Dino and Sauro.'

'Not go to the fair!' cried Mr Watkins. 'Don't be silly, lad. The races are held only once a year and you always spend the afternoon at the fair with the other boys. So be off with you, the coach will be waiting. Keep a look-out as you drive along and I'll make inquiries round here. Somebody must have seen them.'

The fair was one of the highlights of the year and Jed entered into the fun and spent his pocket-money as freely as the others, but he couldn't entirely forget that Dino and Sauro were missing again. Where could they be this time? The Parish Clerk would be furious if he found out. It was a good job he was at the races with Mr Holloway.

The afternoon wore on. All pocket-money had been spent and Jed and his friends drifted round the fair.

Jed was startled when, over the loud-speakers, came an announcement. 'Jed Watkins, please. Is Jed Watkins on the fairground? He's wanted urgently at the racecourse office at the main gate.'

More trouble, thought Jed, running as fast as he could through the crowds. At the office, he found Mr Holloway and several officials waiting impatiently for him.

'Come on, Jed,' urged Mr Holloway. 'The race for the Gold Cup, the most important event, is due to start in a few minutes and – guess what? – Dino and Sauro are making their way on to the course. The Parish Clerk is nearly going mad, poor chap.'

'Where have they been hiding?' Jed inquired, trying manfully to keep pace with the longer-legged grown-ups as they all made their way towards the race track.

'They've apparently been lurking behind trees to the north of the course. I imagine they must have been aware of the horse-boxes passing through the village last night. Some instinct probably led them to come over here to investigate. It's often impossible to understand animals' behaviour.'

They sped along the outside rails bordering the race track. Some of the racegoers, pressed against the rails, were too engrossed watching the line-up of the horses to notice two large bodies looming up behind them. Others, however, glanced over their shoulders and saw the dinosaurs. They scattered hurriedly in all directions, their screams lost among the general hubbub.

The horses were eventually lined up and soon, after a lot of jostling, 'They're off! They're off!' echoed round the course, as the favourite took the lead and raced away. The horses disappeared round the first bend as Jed and Mr Holloway rushed up to the dinosaurs. The Parish Clerk was running round the animals, imploring each in turn to halt.

Arms flapping wildly, the Clerk ran towards Jed. 'Oh, where on earth have you been, Jed?' he wailed. 'Why didn't you come sooner? Stop them! Stop them!'

In spite of all Jed's efforts, however,

Sauro crashed through the rail and he was on the race track. With a backward glance at Jed, Dino followed. People were amazed. Nothing like this had ever happened before. The two beasts, Dino on the stands side and Sauro over on the far side, made their dignified way along the track towards the finishing-post.

'Oh, oh, good heavens! The horses will be coming round the first lap in a minute,'

the Parish Clerk screamed. 'They won't be able to get past. What shall we do? What *shall* we do? I've never been involved in anything so awful in all my life. This is the end. It's just too much. They'll have to ...'

'Oh, that's quite enough. Don't let me hear you say *that* again, for goodness' sake,' cried Mr Holloway impatiently.

'Get off the track, you clumsy great oafs,' yelled the Parish Clerk. 'Oh, oh, I knew it was too good to last. And all this talk of "earning their keep". I hope I'll never, never hear you speak those words again, Mr Holloway.'

But Mr Holloway wasn't paying any attention to the distracted man. Horses, hooves pounding the turf, were rounding the bend. When they saw the dinosaurs ahead of them, the surprised jockeys leaned hard on their stirrups and pulled in the reins. Horses and riders – looking like pygmies behind two giants – fanned out all over the place.

The stands were in an uproar. Jed had a brief glimpse of some very important persons doubled up with laughter as, leading by a short head, Dino ambled in a leisurely manner past the winning-post. Such cheering and shouting had never before been heard on a racecourse. People came down from the stands and surged on to the track, surrounding Dino and Sauro, who had at last halted.

The officials turned to the unfortunate Parish Clerk. 'I hope you realize this is a very, very serious matter, Mr Parish Clerk,' one said. 'Never, in the history of racing, have we experienced anything like this before.'

'And never, in my career as Parish Clerk, has anything like this happened to me before,' groaned the Clerk.

However, after a brief consultation, the officials decided to regard the first race as a false start. Jed succeeded in enticing Dino and Sauro off the track as the horses were lined up a second time. And –

'They're off! They're off!' soon came from all sides again. The dinosaurs seemed to sense the growing excitement and weaved and stretched their long necks towards the royal box, as the horses finished the first lap and disappeared round the bend again.

And it was a proud and happy moment for Jed when, after the race was over, the royal party came down to congratulate Dino on winning the first-ever dinosaur race.

Jed had to lead the animals home once again. He didn't mind. He was very proud and happy. Dino and Sauro had received royal approval, hadn't they? They were becoming more famous every day, weren't they? Never mind what the Parish Clerk had to say about them. He didn't always know when he was well off.

News had spread and all the villagers were out to welcome them home. Jed turned to the Parish Clerk. 'I *told* you they would want to see Dino and Sauro.

Can't imagine anyone not wanting to.
They're the most intelligent and obedient
animals in the world.'